Chicken Little

Pictures by Marjorie Hartwell

A Golden Book • New York

Western Publishing Company, Inc.
Racine, Wisconsin 53404

ISBN 0-307-07022-0 B C D E F G H I J

Once upon a time there was a fluffy chick named Chicken Little.

One day as she scratched for food in the orchard, a little apple fell—*plop*—right on her head.

"Oh!" squealed Chicken Little. "What was that?

"Goodness me!" she cried when she saw the apple. "Oh, the sky has fallen. What shall I do?"

Away ran Chicken Little. She ran so fast she almost bumped into Henny Penny who was just getting off her nest.

"Watch where you are going," warned Henny Penny. "Why are you running, Chicken Little?"

"Oh, Henny Penny!" cried Chicken Little. "The sky has fallen!"

"How do you know the sky has fallen?" asked Henny Penny.

"I saw it with my eyes," said Chicken Little. "I heard it with my ears. And a piece of it fell on my poor little head."

"How awful!" said Henny Penny. "Come, Chicken Little. We must go and tell the king."

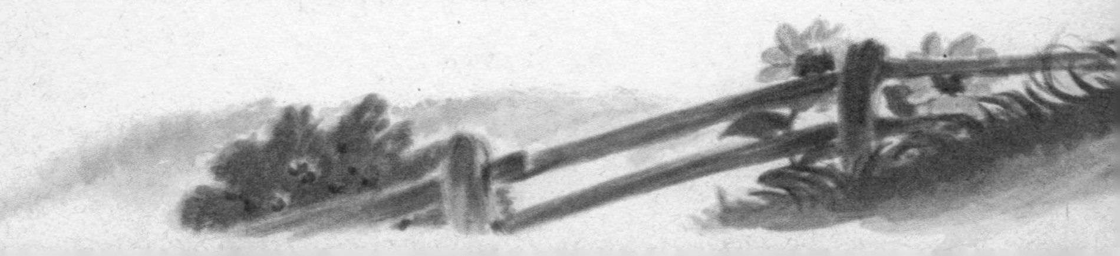

They ran until they met Cocky Locky who was strutting along showing off his beautiful feathers.

"What's the hurry?" asked Cocky Locky, turning his head so they could see his fine red comb.

"Oh, Cocky Locky!" said Henny Penny. "The sky has fallen. We are running to tell the king."

"How do you know the sky has fallen?" asked Cocky Locky.

"I saw it with my eyes," said Chicken Little. "I heard it with my ears. And a piece of it fell on my poor little head."

"How terrible!" cried Cocky Locky. "I'll go along with you."

They ran until they saw Ducky Lucky swimming in the pond.

"Oh, Ducky Lucky!" called Cocky Locky. "The sky has fallen and we are going to tell the king."

Ducky Lucky waddled out of the water. "How do you know the sky has fallen?" she asked.

"I saw it with my eyes," said Chicken Little. "I heard it with my ears. And a piece of it fell on my poor little head."

"Oh, my!" cried Ducky Lucky. "Wait! I'm going with you."

They ran until they met Turkey Lurkey who was spreading his tail into a great big fan.

"Can't you stop for a little visit?" asked Turkey Lurkey.

"Not today!" called Ducky Lucky. "The sky has fallen and we must run to tell the king."

"How do you know the sky has fallen?" asked Turkey Lurkey.

"I saw it with my eyes," said Chicken Little. "I heard it with my ears. And a piece of it fell on my poor little head."

"Of course the king must be told," said Turkey Lurkey. "Follow me and I'll take you to him."

As they ran along they heard a loud, "*Hoo—hoo—hoo!*"

In a tree, Hooty, the owl, blinked his eyes sleepily.

"Don't you know this is my nap time?" he scolded. "What is all the noise about?"

What a clucking and quacking there was as each animal told the owl that the sky had fallen!

"Are you sure the sky has fallen?" asked the owl, blinking first one eye, then the other.

All the animals looked at Chicken Little as she stepped nearer to the owl.

"A piece of the sky fell on my poor little head. See?" she said as she held her head for him to look.

"Hm-mm!" said the owl. "Can you show me the piece of sky that fell, Chicken Little?"

"Oh, yes!" said Chicken Little. "Come with me and I'll show you."

Chicken Little led the way. The owl flew above her and the animals followed in a line.

When they came to the orchard Chicken Little said, "Look! There is the piece of sky that fell on my poor little head."

All of the animals looked at the little apple. Then, one by one, they

walked away—all but the owl.

The wise owl looked at Chicken Little. "That is a little apple from the apple tree," he said. "And if you are a smart little chicken you'll eat it before the others come back to get it."

And that is just what Chicken Little did. She pecked and pecked at it until it was all gone.